# HIS MIRACLE

Happy Reading!
Shaw Hart

# CHAPTER ONE

## Adeline

I laugh as Ryan, Flynn's younger brother, finishes with his story. We're at Aspen's wedding reception and I'm seated across from Aspen and her new husbands. I look over at my friend, my sister, who is sandwiched between her men. Aspen is grinning from ear to ear as she looks between Roman and Flynn. They each have an arm draped over the back of her chair as they gaze down with so much love shining from their eyes that I have to look away. Don't get me wrong, I'm so happy for my friend. She's been through so much and she deserves all of the love and happiness that I know Roman and Flynn will give her.

Losing my parents when I was seven was a rough thing to go through. They were murdered in a home invasion while I was at a friend's house for a sleepover. My parents were both only children and I didn't have any other relatives so I was put in the foster system. That can be an even rougher time and if I hadn't met Aspen when I went to the group home, then I'm not sure that I would be here today. Even if I was, I would still probably be all alone.

I would do anything for Aspen. We've been close since the day we first met and that bond has only grown stronger over the years. When we both turned 18, we left the home and got an apartment together in New York City. Sure, it was a complete dump, but it was ours. No more sharing bathrooms and bedrooms with a dozen other people.

To be fair, our old apartment was really just one big room with barely enough room for the two of us to move around in. We dragged furniture and appliances off the street and furnished our apartment that way. We never did find a bed so the two of us slept on an old mattress on the floor.

When Aspen met Roman and Flynn, we traded our crappy apartment for an Upper East Side townhouse. I figure that once Aspen and the boys get back from their honeymoon I'll move out. I told them a couple of days ago that I was looking for someplace new but they didn't really take it well. Roman and Flynn offered to buy me a place nearby so that I could stay close to Aspen, and while the idea of being close to her is tempting, I don't want to take advantage of them. They told me I could stay and I know they're nervous about me being on my own, but they need their own space right now too. I'm going to stay there while they're on their honeymoon and keep an eye on the place. Once they're back, I'll find a new place and then I'll move out.

I had brain surgery about a month and a half ago and I'm still taking it easy. Truth is, I'm lucky to be alive. A miracle, the doctor's called it. I'm sure I gave Aspen quite the scare when she came home from her night with Roman and Flynn and found me unconscious. I don't really remember much from that day and I know that she doesn't like to talk about it.

I had a tumor on my frontal lobe and was close to dying when Aspen made a deal with Roman and Flynn. One night with her and they would pay all of my medical bills. I owe Aspen my life, but it also got her Roman and Flynn and so she says that we're even.

For the most part, I'm all healed after the surgery. I still get tired easily, but I'm getting stronger every day. I'm back to my job at the animal shelter and my last doctor appointment showed that the tumor hadn't returned.

I look back to Aspen as Flynn leans in and whispers something in her ear. She throws her head back, laughing freely at whatever he said and I watch as Roman looks over at the sound and smiles. That's the kind of love that I want and a pang of jealousy hits me as I watch them. Don't get me wrong, I'm over the moon happy for Aspen. I just wish that I had that too.

I look away from the happy couple and my eyes meet the man seated on my left. Lincoln Hook. He introduced himself to me when he first sat down. He almost tripped over his feet to get to the chair next to me. He hasn't said much since we sat down-but he has been growling anytime anyone pulls my attention away from him.

I've been trying to take him in in little bits out of the corner of my eye. He's got dirty blonde hair that keeps falling in his face. It has a bit to a curl to it and when he pushes it back it curls upward. I can see more of the curl where it hangs around his ears. His moss-green eyes have been glued to me all night and his lips curl upwards every time he catches me looking at him.

It'd be impossible for him not to catch me looking at him. He's been staring at me all night. I can feel his eyes on me even know. Every time I looked over during the wedding, his eyes were on me instead of the happy couple. I could feel him watching me as I mingled with Roman and Flynn's family and friends. He only seems to get upset when I'm around young single guys. I've seen him shooting glares over my head at Ryan every time he says something to me.

Ryan leans in to make a joke about someone further down the table when I hear Lincoln's chair scoot along the floor, closer to mine. I go to turn in his direction when Ryan leans in again. I can feel Lincoln's glare from behind me and a part of me is giddy over his obvious interest. That happiness turns to shock when a hand lands on the back of my chair and I'm dragged to the left.

*Who is this man?*

My eyes snap to Aspen's across the table and I

silently ask her what the hell just happened. Aspen just shrugs but she has the biggest smile on her face. I peer over at Lincoln, wondering what his problem is but he simply smiles at me and hands me a menu, draping his arm over the back of my chair where it sits right next to his. I've been hit on before but never by someone so possessive and obviously interested in me.

"What looks good, my love?" He asks in his deep, smooth, voice.

I don't know if it's the term of endearment or the rumble of his voice as it skitters across my skin, but a shiver makes its way down my spine. I pretend to study my menu and act like I didn't hear his question. He scoots his body closer and now our thighs are pressed together under the table and I'm tucked under his arm. He's got me practically glued to his side. My body feels flushed and I'm sure my face is beet red.

My thoughts are interrupted when the man plastered to my side, leans in and whispers in my ear.

"Are you ok, my love?"

"I'm fine. And I'm not your love." I huff out, trying to scoot away.

"Yes, you are." He says under his breath but since I'm still practically fused with him, I hear him just fine.

The waiters come around and take our orders, bringing out some bread and appetizers. Aspen and her men opted for a very casual wedding, one that suits them all so perfectly. Aspen has never been big on fancy events. Neither am I, for that matter.

I go to grab a roll and some strawberry butter when one is placed in front of me. I look over at Lincoln as he grabs himself one and smears some butter on it. He takes a bite of his before looking over at me.

"Did you want something else, my love?"

"No, this is good." I mumble as I take a bite of my own bread.

The rest of the meal continues in much the same way. The appetizers and bread are passed around and as soon as I so much as glance at something, Lincoln is getting it for me. I finish my water and Lincoln is stopping a passing waiter to ask for more. I stare at him out of the corner of my eye, trying to figure out what his plan is and I see him grin as he watches me right back.

# LINCOLN

I watch as the red blush stains her pale cheeks. I can't stop smiling at her. She's even prettier in person than she is in pictures.

I've been in love with Adeline Monroe since I first looked into her as part of the investigation I did for Roman and Flynn into their now wife. They had contacted me, wanting information on Aspen to try to get her to fall for them and, in the process, I found out about my girl. She was the only real family that Aspen had. The more I found out about Ms. Monroe though, the harder I fell. As soon as I saw a picture of her, I knew that she was mine.

Her narrow face with those unique purple eyes, framed by such long lashes. Her pencil straight black hair that hangs to her chin in a sleek bob. Her full lips are almost always spread in an easy smile. Her high cheekbones divided by that straight nose, with a slight bump in it. I know that she broke it when she was young and she fell off of a tire swing. There isn't much I don't know about Adeline.

I know about her tumor and if Roman and Flynn hadn't paid for the surgery, then I would have. They just beat me to it. I know that she's strong, a fighter, but that she has the biggest heart of anyone I will ever meet. I know she loves Aspen more than anything and I know that she's happy for her but also jealous because she wants a family more than anything. I'm dying to give her all of that. I want to give her anything she needs, anything she wants.

I had it planned out. We would meet at the wedding and I would charm her and ask her to have dinner with me. She would say yes and see immediately that we were meant to be. Real soulmates. Now that I'm sitting next to her though, my brain seems to be going a little haywire. Instead of being charming, I've just been territorial. As soon as Ryan, Flynn's brother, sat down on the other side of her and started talking to her, I saw red. I know Ryan is a good guy but he's stealing her attention. He's making her laugh when it should be me.

I can't seem to force any words out of my tight throat. Every time those fucking gorgeous purple eyes aren't on me, I'm so jealous I can barely see straight but every time her eyes are on me, my mind blanks and all I can think is MINE.

The last time she turned to talk to Ryan, I ended up dragging her into my side and tucking her under my arm. I can hear someone trying to start a conversation with me but there's no way I'm looking away. Not when I have this angel sitting next to me.

Our food arrives and I watch as Adeline digs in. She's too thin but I know that part of that was from before her surgery. She needs to eat more. She seemed to like the strawberry butter a lot and I make a mental note to pick some up for her. I butter another roll with it and put that on her plate. The blush comes back but I get another one of those timid smiles from her.

The waiters clear our plates when we're done and we head back outside where a DJ is set up. I stand next to Adeline as Aspen dances with first Flynn and then Roman. Finally, it's time for the other guests to join in the dancing but before I can ask Adeline if she would like to, Aspen is dragging her out on the dance floor. I stand on the sidelines and watch as Adeline dances with Aspen, then Roman, and then Flynn. Ryan goes to ask her to dance but I can see from her face that she's starting to get tired and I intercept her before he can reach her and lead her over to a table set up outside.

"Let me get you some water, my love." I say as I pull the chair out for her before I head inside to flag down a waiter.

I head back outside with Adeline's water in one hand and a basket of rolls and butter in the other. She's sitting at the table watching all of the other guests dance with a small smile on her face. She looks so relaxed and I want to keep that look on her face at all times.

"Here you are, my love." I say as I place the water and bread in front of her.

"Thanks."

She takes a big gulp of the water but doesn't touch the bread so I go ahead and butter one for her before handing it over to her.

"I'm so full. I seriously can't eat another bite."

She says that but she still brings it to her mouth. I watch her nibble on it as she returns to watching the other couples moving around the dance floor.

"Did you want to dance?" I ask.

"I'm getting pretty tired." She admits and I can see that she hates admitting even this small weakness.

"Then I'll sit with you and keep you company."

I scoot next to her before I lean back in my chair and watch the other guests with her. We sit in companionable silence for a few minutes and I let a satisfied smile stretch my lips when I watch her take the last bite of the roll.

It's getting late and the bride and grooms make the announcement that they're heading for the airport. We all line up and offer congratulations once more before they head for the door.

"Ryan will take you home whenever you're ready to go." I overhear Aspen tell Adeline.

*Hell. No.*

No one is taking my girl anywhere but me.

"I can drive her." I pipe up.

"Oh, I don't want to be an inconvenience." She argues.

"You could never be an inconvenience, my love." I say.

Aspen's eyes are stretched so wide that it's almost comical.

"Besides, I live right across the street from

Roman and Flynn, so it's on my way." I finish.

She looks back to Aspen for confirmation and she just nods back.

"Um, ok. Thank you." She says.

I offer her my hand and she hesitates but finally takes it. I lead her over to my car and open the door for her. I help her into the car before I round the hood and climb behind the wheel.

"All set, my love?"

"Yep."

I merge into traffic and head towards home. I really do live across the street from Roman and Flynn's place, although that's more of a recent development. I know how Adeline and Aspen feel about each other. They're family, sisters, and they won't want to be far apart. I bought the townhouse the day after I did the investigation and I just moved in two weeks ago.

I've been able to watch as Adeline and Aspen leave for work every morning before I follow along after them. I run my own security company so I can set my own hours. I leave every day for lunch when Adeline gets off work and I trail along behind her, making sure she gets home safe. I've been dreaming about the day when I'll get to walk beside her, holding her hand or draping my arm around her shoulders.

Today, I'm going to set us on the path that will get me that dream, will get me my girl.

# CHAPTER TWO

## Adeline

I study Lincoln's hands as he expertly steers the car into traffic. I don't know anyone in New York who has their own car and Aspen and I rarely ride in them. It's cheaper to just take the subway or walk. His car is nice though with buttery leather seats that hug my entire body and enough dials to make it look like we're in a space ship. It's late and traffic isn't too bad so I know we'll be home soon. It's going to be weird staying in Roman and Flynn's house by myself.

"What are you thinking about?"

I'm startled from my thoughts as his deep voice rumbles into the silence that had stretched between us. I clear my throat before answering.

"Just thinking that it's going to be weird staying in Roman and Flynn's house by myself."

"Are you going to be ok? I can stay with you or you can come to my place." He offers instantly.

His concern and obvious protectiveness of

me is refreshing and for a minute I think about taking him up on his offer. It would be nice to not be alone and it's not like it would be a hardship, spending a couple of days with this handsome man. *You barely know him*, my mind whispers.

"I'll be ok." I say.

Lincoln's shoulders drop and he seems disappointed in my answer. Looks like I wasn't the only one who got excited about the idea of us staying together.

Lincoln turns the car onto our street and parks in front of a nice townhouse.

"This is me."

I look up at the dark house but I can't make out much in the moonlight. He wasn't kidding when he said he lived across the street. His house is literally kitty-corner to Roman and Flynn's.

"Did you want to come in?" Lincoln offers and I can hear the hopefulness in his voice.

"It's late and I'm pretty tired, but thanks."

I reach for the car door handle but before I can figure out where the heck it is, Lincoln is out of his side and around to mine. He opens the door easily and offers me his hand, pulling me out of the low seat.

"I'll walk you home."

I expect him to let my hand go but, of course, he doesn't. His fingers interlace with mine as he leads me across the street and up to the front door. I fish in my bag for my set of keys and finally pull them out. I have to shine my phone on the door to find the lock but I finally get the door open.

"Thanks for the ride." I say turning back to him.

I barely finish my sentence when his lips are on mine and he's tugging me into his body. I gasp in shock and he takes the opportunity to push his tongue in my mouth. I stand in shock for seconds before my brain catches up with what's happening. My hand is moving before I realize it and the smack is loud in the quiet night.

He jerks back, stunned, and I use his shock to pull out of his grasp and bolt into the house, locking the door quickly behind me.

"Adeline? Adeline! Shit, I'm sorry. I don't know what came over me."

I lean back against the door, trying to calm my racing heart as he apologizes. It's not that I didn't like him kissing me. He was good at it. Well, I think he was. That was my first kiss and it just caught me off guard. It didn't happen the way I thought it would and I don't know how to feel about that.

I push away from the door and race up the stairs, locking myself in my room. I collapse on the bed and try to catch my breath. I know I should get up and take my makeup off or get changed but it's been a long day and I'm just so tired.

My breathing evens out and I let my eyes slide closed. The last thing I remember before sleep took me, was thinking that my lips still felt like they were tingling.

# LINCOLN

*God, I'm an idiot.*

"Adeline!" I try again.

I've been trying to apologize through the door for five minutes but I don't think she's on the other side anymore. *What have I done?*

To be honest, I'm not even sure what went wrong. She was interested in me. That much was obvious by the way that she looked at me. She let me hold her hand and as I watched her struggle to find her keys and open the door, my heart just kept pounding faster and faster. I've been waiting for this girl for forever and I finally had her in front of me. My brain short-circuited and the next thing I knew my lips were on hers.

It was the single best moment of my life.

And then it wasn't. My hand comes to my cheek and the sting is still there. Damn, my girl can hit. I'm sure I have a red handprint there now.

I moved too fast. I need to get better control of myself when I'm around her. I try to call her name again but when there's no response or movement from the other side of the door, I turn and head for my own house.

I walk inside and the emptiness hits me. It always feels like that when I walk in here. The place is bare. I moved over my essentials but I want Adeline and I to turn this place into a home together. If I have my way, it will be our home very soon.

The lack of décor isn't what makes it feel empty though. It needs to have Adeline in it to feel like home. I want to walk in and hear her laughter, feel her happiness and energy radiating from every room.

I sigh as I trudge up the stairs and into the master bedroom. I kick off my shoes and throw my suit coat on a chair before I collapse face-first on the bed.

Tomorrow. Tomorrow, I'll wake up early and apologize to her again. Then we'll get back on track to our happily ever after.

# CHAPTER THREE

## Adeline

I gasp as the orgasm rolls through me and my eyes pop open to stare at the ceiling. My legs are tangled in the sheets and my bridesmaid dress and my hand is buried in my panties. Lincoln's face flashes through my mind and I remember what I was dreaming of before I woke myself up. I fell asleep quickly but my dreams were filled with images of Lincoln. His lips and hands running over my body, stripping my clothes off piece by piece.

Dream Lincoln licked, kissed and bit his way down my body, paying special attention to my sensitive nipples and the sweet spot beneath my ear. He nipped my clavicle before soothing the spot with his tongue and continuing down my body. When he spread my thighs and started to eat me out, I came. Hard. Well, hard enough to wake me up.

I've touched myself before but I've never come like that before. Most times when I touch myself, I can never quite finish but it would appear that as soon as I picture Lincoln, I'm primed and ready.

My alarm goes off and I jerk my hand out from between my legs, shutting it off and jumping from the bed. I strip my dress off and hop in the shower. I'm going to have to scrub my face to get rid of the makeup that I should have taken off last night.

I hurry through my morning routine and pull on some jeans and my animal shelter shirt. I grab my shoes and head downstairs. I make myself some toast, adding too much cinnamon and sugar to it before shoving my feet in my shoes and my breakfast in my mouth and heading for the door. I lock the door behind me and spin around to find Lincoln standing at the bottom of the stairs.

"Good morning." He says hesitantly.

"Hi." I say around a mouthful of toast.

I walk down the stairs and head down the sidewalk towards work and I'm not surprised when he falls into step beside me.

"I wanted to apologize again for last night. I was an idiot. You just looked so beautiful and I don't think it's a secret that I'm attracted to you."

I don't know what to say so to buy some more time, I shove more toast in my mouth. At this rate, he's going to lose that attraction pretty quick.

"I know I moved too fast and I'm truly sorry if I scared you or," He pauses and I hear him swallow before he finishes. "Or if you feel like I took advantage of you."

"It's not that." I say.

I don't want him to think he took advantage

of me, or that I didn't like his kiss. It just took me off guard.

"Forgive me?" He asks.

"Sure." I say as I reach for the animal shelter door. "Well, thanks for walking me to work. I'll see you later." I say, ducking inside before he can respond.

I go through my usual routine, cleaning out cages and making sure the animals are fed. Lincoln pops into my head over and over again until it's starting to drive me insane. I try my best to push him from my thoughts but it's no use.

I am still having trouble deciphering how I feel about him. Sure, the kiss took me off guard but I knew how he felt about me. He made it obvious all last night. He was so sweet and attentive but I'm just not used to being treated like that.

*He scares you*, my subconscious says. I pause as I realize how true that is. I want a family, what Aspen has with Roman and Flynn so bad, but I'm scared. What if I love like that and something happens? Something like what happened to my parents, and I'm left alone all over again. I'm already so attracted to Lincoln and he's clearly managed to wiggle his way inside of me. It's happening too fast. I need more time.

I spin around, trying to escape my thoughts and run right into someone.

"Oomph!"

Strong hands grip my upper arms and catch me before I can fall backward. I look up into warm brown eyes. The guy holding me smiles down at me before he makes sure I'm settled and lets me go.

"Whoa, sorry about that, uh Adeline." He says as his eyes read my name tag. "I wasn't watching where I was going. Are you ok?"

"Yeah, I'm fine and I'm pretty sure I ran into you so I should probably be the one apologizing." I say as I smile up at him.

This guy is cute with shaggy brown hair and kind brown eyes. His lips curve into a smile as he takes me in and I notice he has a dimple in one cheek. *Nice.*

"I'm Steve and no apology needed. How about you let me buy you dinner to make up for it?"

I study the guy for a minute. He seems kind, and he's obviously polite, not pushy. *He's also not Lincoln.* I shake my head, trying to push that thought away. This guy, he's not Lincoln, but he doesn't make me feel the things Lincoln does either. He's safe.

"I'd love to." I say.

"How about tonight? 7 o'clock?"

"Sounds like fun."

We decide on an Italian place before he says he'll see me tonight and leaves. I go back to work and spend the rest of the day trying to be excited about my date but the truth is, I'd rather it was with Lincoln.

# LINCOLN

I peer through my binoculars into the restaurant. I'm tailing someone, trying to investigate them but I keep thinking about how I missed walking Adeline home today so that I could do this. She looked so pretty this morning but I frown as I think back to how she couldn't seem to get away from me fast enough. *She accepted your apology*, I think.

My client is still eating with his date so I lower the binoculars and sit back in my seat. I check out the restaurant and wonder if Adeline would like to go here sometime. Looks like a good place for a date, all romantic lighting, and intimate seating.

I look up and it's like my mind must have conjured her up. It's like my body is wired to find her. She calls to me, like a light in the darkness, and I'm the moth that is powerless to getaway. I watch as Adeline heads for the restaurant door, pulling it open and disappearing inside. I grab my binoculars and aim them back at the window, only this time I'm looking for my girl.

What is she doing at a romantic place like this? I finally catch a glimpse of her as she crosses the floor and heads to a table tucked away in the back. I have to lean forward to keep her in my eye line and I hear the binoculars creak under my grip when I see some guy stand up from the table and hug her.

*What the hell? Who is that guy*? Adeline is single. It was in my report and I've been following her for weeks. I've never seen this guy before. It must be new. Then it hits me. She's on a date with some other guy and I'm just sitting here? Well, not for long.

I almost rip my car door off in my haste to break up this little date. I run across the street, dodging the traffic and race into the restaurant. I bypass the hostess stand and beeline right for their table. Neither of them looks up as I approach them and my hands tighten into fists when I see her date's eyes flick to her perfect tits.

My girl dressed up for this. Wearing a tight black dress, cut low in the front and ending several inches above her knees. She's got black, four-inch stilettos on and her hair is tied up, exposing her slender neck.

Her date can't seem to keep his eyes off the low-cut front of her dress and I'm already shrugging out of my jacket. I drape it over Adeline's shoulder as I come to a stop next to their table.

"Love." I say, staring down into Adeline's eyes.

Her eyes widen and then I watch as her pupils dilate, the black swallowing up the purple.

"Lincoln, what are you doing here?" She asks.

She tries to push my jacket off but I put my hand on her shoulder, holding it in place.

"I was just walking by and saw you. Mind if I

talk to you for just a minute? Alone?" I ask when neither of them says anything.

I hold my hand out to her and she pauses but finally, takes it.

"I'll be right back." She tells her date.

*Uh, no. won't.*

# CHAPTER FOUR

## Adeline

I follow Lincoln out of the restaurant and when he turns to me, I open my mouth, ready to lay into him. Instead, he grabs my hand and drags me after him. I'm shocked into silence as we cross the road. Where the heck are we going?

That question is answered a second later when he unlocks his car and holds the door open for me. *I guess we're talking in his car*, I think as I slide in. He closes the door and rounds the hood, sliding behind the wheel.

"What did you want to talk about?" I ask.

He starts the car and merges into traffic but doesn't answer my question.

"What are you doing?!? Where are we going?" I ask as I scramble to pull my seatbelt on.

"I'm taking you home."

"No, you're not. I was on a date. I have to go back."

I look behind us as at the restaurant just as he

turns the corner, heading for my house.

"Take me back!" I demand.

He doesn't answer me and I can see his hands tighten on the steering wheel. He's gripping it so tight that his knuckles have turned white.

"I need to go back." I try again.

"No."

That's it. That's all he has to say?

"What is wrong with you? Who do you think you are? You can't just go around kidnapping people!"

"I didn't kidnap you. You willing got in my car."

"Yeah, because I thought that we were just going to sit in it for a minute and talk!"

"I'm not watching you on a date with some other guy. You want to go on a date then it will be with me."

"Not a chance." I spit at him.

He just smiles at me like I'm adorable.

"I would never date you. Steve, my date, he was nice, polite, sweet, everything that you are not. HE is my type, not some brutish, alpha, asshole, who thinks he can tell me what to do."

"I'm your type." He says as he pulls up outside the townhouses, "And you are mine."

"No, you're not." I say as I pull on the door handle, climbing out of the car.

I shoot one last glare at Lincoln before I slam the door closed and start walking down the street. I'm already pulling my phone out to call an uber when strong arms wrap around me from behind and lift me into the air.

I'm carried back to my house and up the stairs before he sets me down. I spin around to face him, ready to rip into him again, but he's already talking.

"Your date? He's probably already left by now. You've been gone for about fifteen minutes; he probably thinks that you're not coming back."

He digs around in my purse, pulling out my keys and unlocking the door for me. I stand there and consider his words and realize he's right. It was our first date and sure Steve was nice but he probably does think that I just ran off with another guy. What a great first date.

I snatch my purse and keys from Lincoln before storming into the house and slamming the door in his face.

# LINCOLN

This door-slamming thing appears to be becoming a pattern. At least she didn't slap me tonight, although she was definitely not happy with me. I suppose I'll owe her another apology tomorrow but this one will be decidedly less sincere. I'll never be sorry for keeping guys away from my girl.

I should head back to the restaurant and continue my surveillance but I'm nervous that Adeline will sneak out and I won't have eyes on her. I cross the street, heading for my own home, as I pull my cellphone out and call my partner.

"Linc."

"Hey Bryson, can you cover surveillance for me tonight? Something came up."

"Sure thing."

I give him the details and tell him I'll see him tomorrow before disconnecting the call. I go upstairs and into the guest room that faces Adeline's room. I've been coming in here since I moved in. It comforts me to know that I only have to look out the window to see where she's at. I sit down on the chair I dragged in here and watch the light across the street.

*God, tonight is going to be a long one.*

Like yesterday, I wait outside of Adeline's

house for her to come out. She pauses when she sees me at the bottom of the steps before she locks the door and heads past me.

*Ahh, the silent treatment today then.*

We walk down the sidewalk together and I take her obvious ignorance to study her features. She's dressed similar to yesterday, only she's wearing a neon pink animal shelter shirt today and black jeans instead of blue. Her hair is pulled up out of her face so I see the scowl she sends my way when she catches me staring.

"You look beautiful."

She just rolls her eyes and tries to walk faster. I'm at least a foot taller than her though and she could never outrun me. She ignores me the entire way to work and I decide to let her cool down some more before I apologize and bring up the idea of us going out on a date. I'll be back when she gets off. I turn and head for my own office, already counting down the hours until I'll see her again.

I end up leaving work early. I don't want her getting off early like yesterday and not being able to walk her home. I wait outside the shelter for twenty minutes and when she still hasn't come out, I decide to go check on things.

I walk inside and immediately spot my girl behind the counter. She looks upset and my guard instantly rises. I will destroy anything that tries to hurt her. She looks up and her eyes lock on mine. I expect her to look pissed but not even the sight of me can chase that sad look away.

I duck behind the counter and into the little office that she's in.

"What's wrong, my love?" I ask, pulling her into my arms.

She melts into my body for a moment and I feel whole. This is what I want, for her to come to me for support or just to lean on. I will always be by her side. I will always be the one to protect her and care for her. No one will ever love her more than I do.

She pulls away from me but her hands still cling to me and my hands still hold her. Her watery purple eyes stare up at me and I want to take that look away.

"What happened? Tell me, my love, and I'll fix it."

"She died." She says and I watch as more tears fall down her cheeks.

"Who? Aspen?" Panic grips me. I can't fix death.

"No. Bonnie."

"Who is Bonnie?"

"This golden retriever mix that we found the other day. She was pregnant and she gave birth but she lost so much blood. Sh-sh-she didn't make it."

"Oh, my love, I'm so sorry."

"No one will take the puppies and we don't have room for them here or the resources to feed them. They're going to put them down if we can't find someone by 5."

More tears flood her eyes and fall down her

cheeks.

"I'll take them." I blurt out.

"What?" She asks, shocked.

I'm just as shocked. What the heck am I going to do with a bunch of puppies? I've never had a dog before but now I'm going to be responsible for a bunch of little ones? It's not even a choice though. I would do anything to make Adeline happy.

"I'll take them. I don't know anything about dogs but I can figure it out and they won't die."

"You would do that?"

"My love, I would do anything for you. Ask and it's yours."

She stares up into my eyes and for a second, I think she's going to kiss me but then another woman walks in and she steps back.

"Marjorie! I found someone to take the puppies!"

I tune out the excited chatter as they talk about what great news that is and I smile as my girl grins up at me. She takes my hand and leads me out of the office and down the hall to a back room.

Inside, the puppies are cuddled up together in a sleeping ball. They look like fleshy lumps but they're kind of cute, I guess. Adeline coos over them as she explains everything that I will need to do to keep these little guys alive.

"Don't worry, I'll come over and help with the feedings or if you have any questions."

"You will?" I ask, surprised by this news.

"Of course. It's the least I can do."

My mind suddenly comes up with fantasies of us getting close and falling in love as we care for these puppies. I want that so bad and suddenly, the idea of adopting eight puppies is a whole lot more appealing.

# CHAPTER FIVE

## Adeline

We leave the shelter and run to the store to grab supplies. I have the list of things that we'll need for the puppies clutched in my hand and we walk into the store together. Lincoln grabs a basket by the door and we head down the aisles. We grab baby bottles and a little kiddie pool, some blankets, and a portable heater. The vet at the shelter told us what we would need and she said she would get us the formula to feed them.

We check out and head back to the shelter. Lincoln leaves to get his car so we can transport them easier. I head inside and the vet shows me how to make their food and feed them. She gives us a box to transport them and once they're fed, I place them inside. Lincoln comes back with the car just as I finish feeding the last puppy. He helps me carry the puppies and supplies back out to the car and we drive home.

I talk about the feeding schedule and what

we'll need to do over the next few weeks. Once they're a month old they can start eating puppy food and we can put them up for adoption. My heart sinks at finding them new homes but I can't afford one dog, let alone eight.

We carry everything inside his house and I take the opportunity to look around.

"Did you just move in?" I blurt out.

The place is bare with only a few necessities, like a couch and tv. His place is set up in much the same way as Aspen's and I already feel like I know my way around. Unlike, Roman and Flynn's place though, Lincoln's feels empty.

"I just moved in two weeks ago. I need to get some stuff though so it will be pretty empty until I can find the time to go to the store and get some furniture. Maybe you can help me with that?" He asks.

"I'm not sure I'd be good at that. I don't really have any experience with decorating."

I think back to my old apartment and how everything inside was just stuff that we found on the streets and carried or dragged back. I wouldn't even know where to start to furnish and decorate a place like this. Lincoln's house is beautiful to start, I would probably just mess it up.

"I think you'd do great and I promise I would love whatever you picked out."

I smile at him as I set the stuff down on the kitchen counter.

"Why don't I rinse the bottles out while you blow up the pool. We can put the blankets in and then the puppies can lay in that instead of that box."

Lincoln leaves to do as I ask and I fill the sink with soap and water, washing and leaving the bottles to dry on the counter. I find Lincoln in the living room. He's got the pool blown up and the blankets spread out on the bottom. He's opening a box of puppy pads when I walk in. I help him spread the pads out on top of the blankets before we place the puppies in.

"Should we name them?" He asks.

"I already have." I admit, sheepishly.

He throws his head back and laughs and the sound is so deep and raspy that is causes butterflies to erupt in my stomach. I press my legs together to try to ease the ache as his eyes find mine again.

"Well? What are they?"

"This little guy is Mowgli, then there's Sasha, Naia, Penny, Neal, Teddy, Mac and Quiche." I say as I point at each small bundle of fur.

"Good names, I don't know how you can tell some of them apart, but I like them."

I cuddle Quiche closer to my chest for a minute before I put him in with his brothers and sisters.

"Think you'll keep one?" He asks.

"I'd keep them all if I could but I could never afford that and I'm looking for a new place. Doubt that it will be big enough for eight dogs and me." I admit.

"They can stay here." He offers.

I just smile as I stare down at the sleeping

puppies. I'm not sure how to respond to that comment. I would love to stay here with Lincoln and the puppies. I'd be so close to Aspen and these houses are amazing, but the real attraction is the man sitting next to me.

"Are you hungry?" He asks after a minute.

"No, not yet. It's a little early for me to eat. Why don't you let me take them home with me tonight and I can do the night time feedings? You can have the rest of the night to yourself." I offer.

"No! It will be such a pain carrying them and all the supplies back and forth every day. Why don't you just stay here? I have plenty of room."

I can't stay in this house with him. I'll maul him! He's too sweet, too attentive, and I can already feel myself falling for him. I need to protect my heart but he's right; it will be a pain to try to move them back and forth like that every day, and multiple times a day at that.

"Looks like I'm moving in then!" I say, trying to make a joke out of it, but the way that Lincoln's eyes flare makes me think that he is determined that it's not just going to be a joke.

# LINCOLN

"Looks like I'm moving in then!"

*I wish.*

I know she means it as a joke but god, I love the sound of that. I love having her in my space. From the second that she walked in the door; this place has come alive. It feels more like home with her here and I'm not sure I can go back to living in this house without her.

"Let's run across the street while the pups are sleeping and grab some of your stuff then."

I hold my hand out to her and help her up from the couch, linking our fingers together as we make our way back to Roman and Flynn's house. Roman and Flynn's place has a similar layout to mine. There's a kitchen, living room, office, and bathroom on the bottom level. All of the bedrooms are upstairs and I follow her up the stairs and into the guest room that she's been staying in.

Adeline walks across the room, pulling the closet open and dragging out a suitcase. She throws it on the bed before going back to the closet and grabbing clothes. She throws in some shirts and jeans before making her way to the dresser and grabbing pajamas and her bra and panties. My cock stiffens when I see flashes of colorful lace and silk. I can't help but picture her wearing just those scraps of lace and nothing else.

I clear my throat and take the opportunity to adjust myself as she ducks down the hall and to the bathroom to grab her toiletries. She comes back in and throws the rest of her stuff in her suitcase before zipping it up and looking around the room to see if she forgot anything.

"I can have movers come over tomorrow and grab the rest of your things." I say as I pick up her suitcase.

"That's ok. The other stuff I don't wear that much so it can stay here."

I frown. I don't want her to have any reason to leave our place, but as I look around, I see that there really isn't that much left here. I can come over later and grab the last of it. I snag her hand with mine as we make our way downstairs. I wait while she locks the front door behind us and then slip her hand back into mine as we make our way home.

"I'm going to check on the puppies. They'll be up soon and we'll need to feed them. I'll start getting the bottles ready."

"I'm just going to run this upstairs and then I'll come help you." I say, motioning to the suitcase.

I take the stairs two at a time, turning into the guest room closest to the master bedroom. I freeze when I walk in and realize that there's one big problem. The room is empty.

I hadn't been kidding when I asked Adeline for help decorating and furnishing the place. I hadn't thought about my lack of furniture when I invited her to stay here. I just wanted to be close to her, to have her in my space.

I go next door and place the suitcase in the master bedroom before I head downstairs. I find Adeline in the kitchen, already making the puppy's next bottles. She's just finishing the last one when I walk in.

"Perfect timing."

She turns and smiles at me and my heart flips over in my chest. She hands me four of the bottles and grabs the other four before we head into the living room. The puppies are starting to wiggle around in the pool and we sit down next to it. Adeline shows me how to properly feed the puppies and then we each grab one.

"Which one is this?" I ask.

"Quiche." She says with a smile.

I try to learn their names as we feed them and Adeline helps by pointing out several differences with their fur and eyes. Her stomach growls as we lay the last puppy down and we decide to order a pizza.

Adeline washes the bottles while I order the food. I switch out the puppy pee pads while we wait for the food to get here. Adeline comes back in right as the doorbell rings. I pay for the food and take it into the kitchen where Adeline is trying to find dishes.

"Where is everything at? Did you not unpack the dishes yet?" She asks, amused.

"I don't have any. I've just been eating off of paper plates or take out containers.

She thinks this is funny and throws her head back as she laughs at me. I'm not used to anyone laughing at me but when she does it, I feel an answering smile tugging at my lips.

"I told you I needed to get stuff!" I try to defend myself.

"Ok, we need to go get you some of the basics tomorrow then."

I grab the paper plates and set them on the counter next to the pizza as Adeline grabs some bottles of water from the fridge. There's no table or chairs so we take the food back into the living room.

"Speaking of needing furniture, I forgot that there's nothing in the guest rooms. Even the master bedroom just has a mattress. You can have the master though and I'll sleep on the couch."

She looks at me and then at the couch that we're sitting on and I know what she's thinking; there's no way I'm fitting on this couch. Even if I could, the couch is a couple of years old and you can feel the springs in some places. I'm not looking forward to cramming myself onto it tonight, but if it means that Adeline is here with me, then I'll suck it up.

"I can take the couch. I'm smaller than you so it would probably be more comfortable for me."

"No, no, I'll be fine. The couch is pretty lumpy."

She doesn't look happy about it but she lets

the subject drop. We finish eating and clean up the mess, putting the food away and throwing out the paper plates. I show her upstairs and to the master bedroom.

She walks into the room and I follow after her. As soon as I see her in here, a feeling of completeness settles over me. *I need this girl.*

She looks over to the mattress on the floor. I want her to be happy here. With me. I had a bed but I wanted Adeline to pick out our bed. The bed we share will be with us for years. It will be where we make love, where our children are conceived, where I will fall asleep every night with her in my arms and wake up every day to see her lying next to me.

"This reminds me of Aspen and my old apartment."

"This room?"

"No, the mattress on the floor. We couldn't afford anything else so we dragged some mattress in off the streets and shared it. I kind of miss it. Is that crazy?"

"No, love. You two are close. Her getting married and moving has to be a big change."

She's lost in thought for a minute before she looks back to me.

"It's a king, right?"

"The mattress? Yeah."

"Then it should be big enough for the two of us. That way you won't have to sleep on the lumpy couch."

"Are you sure?" I ask but I can tell that I'm

doing a terrible job of keeping the excitement out of my voice.

"Yeah. It will be fine and we can get some furniture or an air mattress tomorrow."

I was looking forward to shopping with her tomorrow because it would mean that she was starting to leave her touch on our home but now that it would mean that she wouldn't be sleeping next to me, I'm decidedly less enthusiastic.

"Mind if I take a shower? Then we can feed the pups and get some sleep. We'll probably have to get up two or three times tonight."

"Sounds good, love."

She grabs her toiletry bag and I show her to the connecting bathroom. I leave her to shower and head back downstairs. I return some work emails and a couple of texts from Bryson, my business partner, and best friend, before Adeline comes back downstairs. I just about swallow my tongue when I take her in. Her face is free of makeup and her hair is damp and brushed away from her face. She's wearing a pair of sleep shorts that are rolled at the waist. They're so short that I wonder if I'll be able to see her ass if she turns around. She's wearing a light pink camisole that's molded to her torso, showing off her perfect tits and lack of bra. I'm rock hard and my phone slips from my hand as I watch her bare legs and feet make their way over to me.

I can feel my jeans strangling my cock as I help her make the bottles and we feed the puppies one more time before we head to bed. I'm pleased when I can recognize most of the puppies. I mix up Mowgli and Neal but they're the most similar.

We put the puppies down for the night and climb the stairs to head for bed. She's already in her pajamas and I slip into the closet to change. Normally, I sleep naked but I'm not sure how she would react to that. I take my jeans and shirt off but leave my boxers on before I head back out to her. She's already under the covers and I pause before turning off the lights to take her in. She's perfection.

I turn the light off but turn the bathroom light on and leave the door cracked. That way we can see when we get up to feed the puppies in a couple of hours. Plus, I'll be able to see her still.

I pull the covers back and crawl onto the mattress next to her. For the first time in my life, I wish that I had a smaller bed. I would give anything to feel her pressed up against me right now.

"Goodnight, Linc." She says as she rolls over onto her side.

"Goodnight, love." I say as I lay down next to her.

# CHAPTER SIX

## Adeline

I wake the next morning to find the mattress next to me empty. We got up a couple of times last night to feed the puppies and change the blankets in the pool. Each time we got more and more comfortable with each other. I could feel his eyes on me as I moved around in just my pajamas and I grew damp between my legs every time I caught him checking me out.

I had been a little self-conscious when I had first come downstairs in my pajamas but when his eyes had practically devoured me, that self-consciousness had turned to lust. The way he looked at me, made me feel powerful and desirable. We had fed the puppies and then gone to bed and when I woke up several hours later for the first feeding, Lincoln was wrapped around me. I smiled to myself, secretly loving that he was drawn to me, even in his sleep.

I roll out of bed, wondering if Lincoln is already up and feeding the puppies. I think about changing but I want to see him admiring me some more. I slip from the room and head downstairs but I don't find him with the puppies or in any of the rooms. I'm about to make another pass when the front door opens and Lincoln walks in carrying a paper bag and two coffee cups.

"Hey, I was wondering where you went."

"Did you miss me, love?"

He hands me one of the coffee cups and I take a drink, avoiding his question. I'm expecting coffee, which I don't really like but I can choke it down. I'm surprised when I drink and realize that it's hot chocolate.

"Hot chocolate?" I ask.

"Yeah, that's what you like, right?"

"Yeah, but how did you know?"

"I pay attention to you, love."

I smile as I turn away, taking another drink.

"I got some bagels. I thought that we could eat before we have to feed the puppies."

He pulls a bagel out for me and I take a bite of it. We lean against the counter as we eat and I watch as his eyes run over me. I can feel my nipples tighten into hard peaks and he moans as his eyes land on them. I watch as he licks his lips and his eyes trace over my body, memorizing every dip and curve.

The puppies start to whine and I take my last bite of bagel and head over to the sink to make their bottles. I feel Lincoln come up behind me and his front presses against my back as we stand at the sink. I can't help myself and I rub my butt back and forth against his erection. His hands land on my hips and he holds me steady as he pants into the back of my neck.

His breath causes shivers to race down my spine. I moan as he places a wet kiss where my shoulder meets my neck. I tilt my head, giving him more room, and his mouth latches onto my neck sucking and nipping until he reaches below my ear. He rubs his cock against my behind. It feels like I'm burning up inside and my panties are so soaked that they're sticking to me.

The puppies cry louder and it jerks us out of our embrace. Lincoln clears his throat and steps away from. I look at him out of the corner of my eye and see him adjust himself with a pained look on his face. My own face is so hot that I know it must be tomato red.

We take the bottles into the living room and make quick work of feeding the puppies and changing the blankets and pee pads.

"I'll take care of the bottles. Why don't you go ahead and get ready for work?"

"Ok."

I leave him in the kitchen before I head upstairs and take a shower, quickly drying off and getting dressed. We talked about it yesterday and Lincoln will be in the office today so he's going to take the puppies in with him.

I tug my shoes on and head downstairs, helping him get the puppies and the bottles he'll need today packed up. We carry everything out to the car and he drives me to work. We exchange phone numbers, so if he has a question or needs help, he can call me.

"I'll pick you up this afternoon, love." He says as I hop out.

"Have a good one. Let me know if you need anything."

"I will."

I slam the car door and wave before heading into work. I should use this time to cool off from our session in the kitchen, but it's all that's running through my head. Normally, I love my job and being at the shelter but today, I just want to be back home with him.

# LINCOLN

**Lincoln:** How's work?
**Adeline:** Good. How about you? How are the puppies doing?
**Lincoln:** All good. We miss you.

I grip my phone tighter, willing her to respond, to tell me she misses me too. It beeps and I slide my finger across the screen.

**Adeline:** Only a couple more hours and I'll be there.
**Lincoln:** Can't wait, love. I'm counting down the seconds.

I put my phone away and try to focus on work. My assistants have been cuddling the puppies all morning and they just helped me feed them and put them down. They're all in their pool now sleeping. I have to admit, I wasn't that excited about taking care of eight puppies, but they've grown on me.

Bryson walks in and sits down across from my desk. He raises his eyebrows at me when he sees the puppies. I forgot he was out on surveillance and so he didn't know that they were here.

"Long story." I say.

"Adeline?"

Ok, maybe not that long of a story. Bryson knows me too well and he knows how I feel about Adeline. He's been helping me with keeping an eye on her. He's my best friend and the only person I feel comfortable letting near my girl.

"Whatcha got for me?" I ask, changing the subject.

He hands me some papers and I scan through them. It's a bunch of apartment listings and some ads from guys looking for roommates. I look up confused.

"Adeline has been looking at them. Should I start vetting the roommates?"

My fist curls around the papers, crumbling them in my hand.

"No."

He smirks at me as he stands and leaves my office. Bastard knew I wasn't going to let her leave.

I'll need to put a stop to this. No way is my girl living with some other guy. She's definitely not living in one of these apartments. They're all run down or in sketchy neighborhoods. I pull my phone back out, shooting off another text to her.

**Lincoln:** Why are you looking for new apartments?
**Adeline:** How do you know that I am?
**Lincoln:** Told you, love, I pay attention to you.
**Adeline:** I figure that Aspen and the boys are going to want their space once they get back.
**Lincoln:** You could move in with me.

She doesn't answer and I know that she

won't.

**Lincoln:** Promise you won't leave me before the puppies are old enough to be adopted?
**Adeline:** I promise.

I settle back in my chair, running my fingers through my hair. One month. That gives me one month to get her to fall in love with me, to agree to marry me and spend the rest of our lives together.

Shouldn't be that hard, right?

# CHAPTER SEVEN

## Adeline

Three Weeks Later...

Lincoln comes up behind me, leaving a noisy kiss on my cheek. He must have just gotten back from taking the puppies outside. We've been slowly starting to potty train them and every morning Lincoln takes them all out while I make us breakfast. I laugh as I finish stirring my hot chocolate and join him at the kitchen table.

The table just got here a couple of days ago. We went around and ordered furniture for most of the house the first week I was here and they have slowly been delivered. Now the house is almost completely furnished. The only rooms that aren't done are the guest rooms. Lincoln said that he wasn't sure what he was going to use the rooms for. He was talking about making one of them a gym and kept putting off finding furniture for them. I think that he just said that because he wanted me to sleep in his room with him. By the time the guest beds would have arrived, I would be getting ready to leave so I didn't push too hard.

I'd never admit it to him but I love falling asleep with him every night. The night time feedings have gone down and now I get to spend the whole uninterrupted night wrapped in his arms. The first week of us sharing the bed, we would fall asleep on separate sides but we always woke up wrapped around each other. By the second week, Lincoln just said screw it and pulled me into him. I've gotten so used to sleeping like this, that I'm not sure I'll be able to sleep without him molded to me. I can feel the heat from his naked chest through my thin sleep shirt, his bare legs tangled with mine, and the weight of his arm where it wraps around my waist. It's all comforting to me.

It's also a huge turn on. I have a hard time trying to hide my pebbled nipples from him and sometimes I wonder if he can tell how wet he makes me. Everything this man does is a turn on for me. His handsome face and the way his hair hangs over his forehead. His piercing green eyes and the way they always seem to be trained on me. Feeling his ripped body pressed up against me every night. All of it gets me so hot.

It's more than that though. He's so sweet to me, always making sure that I have everything that I need and checking in with me throughout the day. He lets me pick dinner every day and sends me lunch on the days that he can't come to the shelter and bring me something.

He's so protective of me too. He walks close to me whenever we go out and makes sure that no one jostles me. We spent one night early on talking and he told me about his time in the navy and how he decided to get out and start his own security company with his friend. Now it's one of the biggest in the country, with a waitlist and government contracts. I told him about my tumor and growing up in the foster system with Aspen.

The way he treats me turns me on but watching him with the puppies is what caused me to fall in love with him. He's so patient with them. I know that having eight puppies running around and barking is a lot but he seems to take it in stride. He never complains about having to take them to work every day. I know that if I said I wanted to keep them all, he wouldn't even hesitate. It's like he lives to make me happy. How could I not fall for him?

The only problem is he hasn't tried anything. Sure, he holds my hand and kisses my cheek or head. He dotes on me and I've never seen him so much as glance in another girl's direction, but he hasn't tried to take things further with us.

Aspen got back from her honeymoon last night and I'm headed over there today. Maybe she'll have some advice for me.

## LINCOLN

I hate that Aspen is back. I know that's selfish. She's Adeline's best friend, her family, but now I have to share my girl. Adeline is across the street right now and I'm at our house with the puppies. I keep pacing in front of the window, trying to catch a glimpse of her, hopefully when she's headed back to me.

The puppies are chewing on toys and wresting in the front room. They only have a week left before they'll be old enough to eat regular puppy food and then Adeline will be leaving me.

I've been trying to go slow with her. To show her that we're perfect together and meant to be but she's a hard one to read. She lets me touch her and hold her hand or cuddle her when we're sleeping or watching tv on the couch. I've kissed her cheek or her head but she hasn't given me any sign that she wants to take things further.

I'm starting to go insane and I know most of it is just panic at her leaving but I don't know how to get through to her. I would do anything, be anyone, if she would just love me. I want to tell her that I'm in love with her so bad. Every morning when I wake up with her next to me, I want to tell her. Every night when she scoots closer to me and sighs as I wrap my arm around her before we fall asleep, I want to tell her. There are a million different times during every day that I have to hold myself back from blurting it out.

My pacing is interrupted by the front door opening. I see Adeline walk in with a smile on her face and I'm next to her in a second.

"You're back."

"Yeah, Roman and Flynn got home and couldn't keep their hands off Aspen so I took that as my cue to leave."

"How is everyone?"

"Happy. In love. Tan." She finishes with a little laugh.

"I'm glad they're back. I know you were missing Aspen."

"It's still weird being away from her and I think that was the longest we went without talking."

"You two texted while she was gone though."

"Yeah, but it's not the same as seeing her face to face and talking. She's so happy and she deserves it. Although, I will admit I'm a little jealous of her tan. I would kill to go to some tropical island for vacation."

"Name the place and I'll take you there, love."

The image of Adeline running around in just a swimsuit, smiling at me as we lay in the sun together flashes in my head. Sounds like the best vacation ever to me. She just smiles at my offer.

"How are the pups doing?"

"Good. They're running around like little maniacs."

Quiche chooses that moment to scamper in and jump all over us. He is Adeline's favorite and I already know that I'll be keeping him. Hell, if she wants all of the puppies, then we'll keep them all.

"Hey there, buddy!"

I watch as Adeline leans down to pet the dog and he wastes no time in licking her face. *Lucky dog.*

"It's almost time to switch you guys to puppy food."

My smile drops from my face as I think about our time together being almost over.

"We should pick up food for them soon."

"Right. Why don't you order some? You know what kind is best for them."

My phone rings and I walk into the other room to answer it as she pulls her own phone from her pocket to order the puppy food.

"My wallets on the counter. Use my card to pay for it, ok?"

"Ok." She calls as I walk out of the room.

I answer my phone. It's just Bryson with a question about one of our clients. I hang up with him and head back to the kitchen to find Adeline there. She's standing like she's frozen as she holds my wallet.

*Shit.*

I know exactly what has caused that look.

# CHAPTER EIGHT

## Adeline

I grab Lincoln's wallet from the counter, opening it to grab his credit card when I freeze. Inside his wallet is some cash and cards and... a picture of me from when I was younger. The air catches in my lungs.

Why does he have this? Where did he even get it? The picture is of Aspen and I when we first moved into our old apartment. I'm pretty sure we only had one copy of this picture so how does he have one?

My mind keeps jumping from one question to the next. I can't focus on anything. I stand there frozen. What does this mean? He told me that he paid attention to me and at the time I just thought he meant he watched when we were together but now? Is he stalking me? I never showed him this picture. *He knew that you were looking for apartments*, my mind whispers as more doubts flood me.

"Adeline?"

My eyes snap up to meet Lincoln's and he

walks towards me. I step back quickly, dropping his wallet between us.

"Let me explain, love. Please." He says as he steps over it.

He doesn't even glance at it as he steps over it.

"How? How did you get that picture? Why was it in your wallet? Are you stalking me? You said that you pay attention to me. Oh my god! What is going on?" I cry.

"I found it when I moved the rest of your stuff. I-, you just looked so beautiful, so happy. I'm sorry."

I back up further and further and he keeps pace with me.

"Adeline, love, please, let's just sit down and I can explain better."

"I can't."

I spin and rip the door open, running across the street and back to Aspen's. Luckily, they're upstairs when I race inside. I throw the door closed and lock it behind me before sprinting up the stairs and back into my old room. I throw myself on the bed and that's when I realize that tears are streaming down my face. I fall back on the bed and cry until finally, Aspen knocks on the door and lets herself in.

"Addy? Are you ok?"

There's a knock at my bedroom door and Roman pokes his head in.

"Lincoln is downstairs. He wants to talk to Adeline."

"No." I say.

Aspen looks at me before turning back to her husband.

"Not now. Tell him to go away."

Roman nods to her, before giving me a worried look and closing the door.

"What happened?" She asks.

"Lincoln. I think he's been stalking me."

She snorts as she sits on the bed next to me.

"Yeah, that dude is obsessed with you but in a sweet way. He's totally in love with you. I don't think he would ever hurt you though. Roman and Flynn both like him and they love you. They wouldn't let him near you if they thought he would hurt you."

I tell her what happened when I got home. About him saying he would take me anywhere I wanted to go, seeming upset when I mentioned the puppies would be on real food soon, and finally, finding our picture in his wallet. I tell her about how he kept saying that he pays attention to me and the way that he broke up my date. We talk about how he knew about the apartments that I was looking at.

We talk and talk and try to work through things but in the end, I still don't know how to feel about all of this.

"Yes, you do. You love him too. You're just scared to let him in. You're scared that he'll leave you like your parents did but Addy, that guy worships you. He's not going anywhere."

"Can I stay here tonight?" I ask.

"Of course. You know you're welcome here anytime."

She hugs me close before she gets up and leaves the room. I curl up on my side, trying to sort through everything in my head one more time.

I'm not sure when I fall asleep, but when I wake up the sun is starting to rise. I check my phone and see a bunch of missed calls and texts from Lincoln. I ignore them for now. I have to get up and get ready for work and I don't want to get dragged down into everything right now.

I run into the bathroom and try to finger comb my hair. None of my stuff is here so that will have to do. When I walk out into the hallway, Aspen is there.

"Morning."

"Morning. Think I can borrow some toothpaste?"

"Yeah, I have some clean clothes for you too."

She pops back into her bedroom and comes out with a folded animal shelter shirt and a pair of my jeans. My toothbrush and comb are on top of the pile too. All of this was over at Lincoln's place.

"How?" I start.

"Lincoln brought it over. Said he wanted you to have what you would need in the morning." She says with a told you so smirk.

I don't say anything to that, just grab the pile and head back into the bathroom. She follows me inside and sits on the counter. I smile at that. We used to have to crowd into the bathroom at our old place but here there's so much room that we can both fit comfortably.

"You know, it's nice that he lives right across the street. Convenient."

"Yeah, he just moved in like a month ago." I say.

"Hmm, wonder why he decided to move here?" She asks but she's saying it in a voice like she already knows the answer.

"Me." I say as I realize that she's probably right.

He knew that Aspen and I were close and so, of course, he would move close to her. For me. God, he really must love me. My phone goes off and I see it's another text from Lincoln.

**Lincoln:** Good morning, my love.

I debate if I should respond and another message comes in.

**Lincoln:** Let me walk you to work?
**Adeline:** I need more time.

Even I'm disappointed in my answer but what Aspen said last night was true. I am scared and I just need a little more time to deal with it.

# LINCOLN

**Adeline:** I need more time.

I sigh as I drop my phone down next to me. I barely slept last night. The house just felt empty without her in it and every time I would roll over, I would reach for her and she was never there.

I drag myself from bed and take the puppies outside before I make them their bottles. Even Quiche seems sad that Adeline isn't here.

"I know, buddy." I say as I bend down to scratch his ears. "Don't worry, I'm going to get her back."

Once the puppies are all set, I run upstairs to get ready for work. I don't have much on my docket for today so I just dress casually in jeans and a t-shirt. I leave my house and see that Adeline and Aspen have already left theirs. I can see them walking a couple of feet ahead of me.

She said she needed time before I could walk her to work but she didn't say I couldn't follow her to work. I know that's obsessive but I just have this need to know that she's ok.

I keep my distance and trail after them as they walk to the animal shelter. I stay at the corner as they say goodbye and I watch Adeline walk into work. It's only been one night but I miss her so much already. It feels like my world is crumbling around me.

I spend the morning at the office, trying to focus on work and not on what Adeline is doing. At eleven, I give up and head to the animal shelter. I didn't see her carrying a lunch and I've been stressing, wondering if she's hungry, all morning.

I stop at the deli down the street from the shelter and grab her favorite sandwich. I'll just take this to her and then maybe I can explain the photo again and try to apologize. Hopefully, we can get this relationship back on track.

# CHAPTER NINE

## Adeline

"Hey, Addy. There's a man here to see you." Carol says with a knowing smirk.

She winks at me before she goes back to work. I know who the man here to see me is before I even go to the front. Lincoln. I should have known he wasn't going to give me time. Well, not much of it anyways.

I walk out of the back and see him standing by the front desk with a brown paper bag in his hand. He looks like he didn't sleep last night. He's dressed casually in jeans a t-shirt and a pair of sneakers. His hair is mussed and his eyes look tired, with dark circles under them.

"I brought you lunch, love."

"Thanks." I say as he hands me the bag.

We stand in awkward silence as we stare across the desk at each other.

"It's your favorite, from the deli across the street."

"Great. Thanks again."

"Can we talk?" He blurts.

Something about how vulnerable he looks when he asks makes me lower my guard. I want to stay mad at him but the more I think about it, the more I start to soften. I wanted someone to love me the way that Roman and Flynn love Aspen and I've been pushing him away and keeping him at arm's length from the beginning.

Lincoln cares about me. He constantly worries about me and if I have everything I need, if I'm safe and taken care of. He does everything in his power to make me happy, from adopting eight puppies, to offering to take me on a vacation.

I know that Lincoln loves me. He's made that clear from the beginning. I know that Lincoln would never leave me. Not by choice, anyways. Now I just need to give up this fear. I need to take a chance on this with him because I think it's everything that I've wanted in my whole life.

"Not here. Can you pick me up after work? We can talk at home."

"Home?" He asks and I've never seen him look so excited.

"Yeah. At home."

I lean up on my tiptoes and kiss his cheek.

"I'll see you after work. Thanks for the sandwich."

I look at him one last time before I head back into the back.

## LINCOLN

I head back to the office to pick up the puppies before I head back to the animal shelter to pick up Adeline. She's waiting out front when I pull up and she slides in before I can hop out to get her door.

She turns around and coos at the puppies as they try to jump all over her. She laughs as Quiche climbs up on the center console to lick her face.

"I missed you too, guys." She laughs as she tries to pet all of them at once.

The ride home is pretty quick and soon I'm pulling up out front of the house. She helps me get all of the puppies inside and we both collapse on the couch. She laughs as we watch them run over to their toys and start to play almost instantly.

"I love you."

Her laughter cuts off abruptly as she looks at me with wide eyes. *Yeah, maybe I shouldn't have just blurted it out like that...*

"I've loved you since the first moment that I saw you. Roman and Flynn hired me to investigate Aspen. They were trying to get her to go out with them but she wouldn't give them the time of day. They wanted to know if she was seeing someone else but instead of finding a boyfriend, I found you. I started keeping an eye on you then. I knew you were sick, that you had a tumor and needed surgery and I was about to offer to pay for it when Roman and Flynn did instead. I never would have let anything happen to you, love. I've been trying to get you to see how perfect we are together. That I would do anything for you. All I want is for you to be happy but I really want to be the one who makes you happy. I know you might need more time but I just need to know, will you ever give me a shot? Give US a shot?"

# CHAPTER TEN

## Adeline

I stare wide-eyed at Lincoln as his declaration spins around in my head. This is it. My heart beats wildly in my chest as I look up into his eyes.

"Yes." I whisper but I'm not sure that he heard me.

I have to clear my throat to try again.

"Yes, I can give you, this, a chance."

"Oh, Adeline."

The next thing I know, I'm being crushed in his arms.

"You have no idea how happy that makes me. How happy you make me."

I cuddle into him further as his arms stay locked around me. We stay like that for several long minutes before the dogs start barking and we pull apart.

"Why don't we order some food? I can take the dogs outside and then we can feed them before the food gets here."

"Sounds perfect."

He stares at me for a second and then he leans down towards me. His lips stop a breath away from mine but I can feel his warm breath as it skates across my lips. His eyes meet mine, looking for permission. I look up at him and lick my lips before I close the distance between us.

His lips are warm and firm against mine. His hands come up to cup my face and I feel his tongue as it licks against my lips, seeking entrance. I moan as my lips part and his tongue pushes in. I hesitate before slowly stroking my tongue against his. He groans and it emboldens me. I tunnel my hands into his hair and pull him closer to me.

"Ruff!"

A little ball of fur launches at us and we break apart as it pushes between are bodies. Lincoln scowls down at Quiche and that just makes me laugh harder. Lincoln sighs but as I keep laughing, he smiles at me.

"Hamburgers?" He asks.

My stomach growls and I nod my head.

"With milkshakes?" I ask.

"Anything for you, my love."

He pulls out his phone and orders our dinner while I get the dogs hooked up on their leashes. We take them outside and let them do their business. The dog food should be delivered tomorrow and we only have two more days until they can be off the bottled food and onto puppy chow.

We herd them all back inside and Lincoln

helps me make the bottles. We just finish feeding them when the doorbell rings and I finish up with the puppies while Lincoln pays for the food.

We talk and eat and Lincoln lets me drink half of his milkshake and steal some of his fries. I tell him stories about growing up with Aspen and he tells me stories about his time in the navy and some of his funnier investigation stories.

The next time I look away from his eyes, the sun has set. We've been talking for hours and the puppies are starting to get hungry again. We feed them one last time before laying them down for the night.

"Are yo- will you spend the night?" He asks.

"Yeah."

"Yeah?"

"Well, I mean that all of my stuff is still here, so it would probably be easier." I say, pretending that I'm not dying to spend the night wrapped in his arms.

I follow him up the stairs and we get dressed and ready for bed together. We fall back into the same routine as before so easily. I climb under the covers and he hits the lights before he slides in on his side.

He wastes no time in wrapping me up in his arms and kissing the top of my head. I drift off to sleep quickly, feeling safe and at home in his arms.

# LINCOLN

I wake feeling rested with Adeline sprawled across my chest. My arms are wrapped tight around her as she sleeps on top of me. I stroke my hand down her hair as I feel her chest rise and fall against mine. I would give anything to wake every morning just like this.

She starts to stir in my arms and I lay still as she leans up on her arms and looks down at me.

"Morning." She says sleepily.

She smiles down at me and I return it.

"Morning, love."

I brush some loose hair out of her face and she surprises me by leaning down and pressing her lips against mine. I grip her hips as her legs spread wide on either side of my legs. Her arms twine around my neck and her hips grind down against my hard length. She moans as it aligns with her center and she pushes harder against it.

I groan as she rocks her hips harder against me. I want to take control of her movements but the knowledge that she's using me to get herself off is so hot that I just freeze and let her set the pace.

She rubs back and forth, grinding down harder as her clit rubs against me. Over and over again. I can feel her heat through her sleep shorts and my thin boxers. She's wet and a few spurts of come spill from my cock as I realize how turned on she is.

"That's it, love. Use me. Show me how it's done."

She moans as she rocks once more, grinding down hard at the base of my cock.

"Lincoln!"

Hearing her scream my name as she comes all over me, sets me off. I come with her, spilling into my boxers. She continues to rock against me as her orgasm plays out. We collapse back onto the bed together, both panting.

"Adeline, that was- WOW." I say when I calm down.

I look over to see her blushing.

"Let me taste you." I say, already leaning up.

I want to spread her out on this bed and lick and taste every inch of her. Her shorts must be a mess, but I could help clean her up. I reach for the hem of her tank top when our alarms go off.

We both groan as we reach over to switch them off. She climbs out of bed before I can stop her and I watch as she grabs some clean clothes and heads into the bathroom. I roll out of bed after her but head down to the kitchen. I make the puppies their bottles and put some bread into the toaster for Adeline. She loves toast with cinnamon and sugar for breakfast.

I hear her come down the stairs behind me and I hand her the toast as I kiss her head. I run upstairs to pull on some clothes before I come back down and help Adeline with the puppies. We take them outside and then load everyone into the car and head to the shelter.

I pull up outside of her work and she turns to me.

"Thanks for the ride."

"Anything for you, love. I'll pick you up after work?"

"Ok."

She reaches for the door handle but there's something that's been on my mind.

"Wait!"

She turns to look at me.

"I've been thinking and well, I was wondering if you would go out on a date with me?"

"I would love to."

She smiles at me and I swear everything is right in the world. I put the car in drive. I need to get to work. I have a date to plan.

# CHAPTER ELEVEN

## Adeline

The day drags as I wait for Lincoln to pick me up. I've been trying to guess what he has planned for our date tonight all day. I finish up at the shelter and then head outside. Lincoln and the puppies are pulling up right when I get outside.

He goes to get out of the car, I'm sure to open the door for me, but three dogs take that opportunity to jump over the seat. I laugh as he tries to hold them all back and I open the car door to help him. I gently push them back as I crawl into my seat.

"Hey." I say, still laughing.

Quiche climbs onto his lap and licks his face. I grab Quiche and drag him off of Lincoln and into my lap.

"Hey, buddy." I coo, "Where's my kisses?"

"Nope!"

Lincoln's outburst startles me and I look over at him with wide eyes.

"What?"

"If anyone is giving you kisses, it's me." He grumps.

"You're ridiculous." I laugh.

He scowls at Quiche as I place him in the back-seat with the others. I sit back in my seat and he leans over to me, brushing his lips against mine.

"I missed you, love." He says.

I can feel the stupid grin split my face and I kiss him back.

"I missed you too." I admit.

He grins back at me and puts the car in drive, heading home.

We pull up outside our home and I see Aspen, Roman, and Flynn waiting outside. I look questioningly at Lincoln.

"I asked them to watch the puppies tonight while we go out."

My heart melts. I didn't even think about what we would do with the puppies but Lincoln is always thinking ahead for us. I lean across the seat and give him another quick kiss before I climb out and help him corral the puppies.

We bring them over to Aspen's house before making another trip to get their bed and bottles. Once everything is all set at their house, we say goodbye and head back over to our place. I pause. *Our place.* I don't know when I started thinking about it like that but it feels right. It feels like home.

"Why don't you go get ready, love?"

"Where are we going?"

"It's a surprise." He says cryptically.

"How should I dress?"

"Wear whatever you want, love. You'll always be perfect."

I blush before I skip past him and up the stairs to our room. I don't have that many dressy clothes; I've never needed too. So instead I put on a pair of clean black skinny jeans and a flowered tunic over a black tank top. I slide my feet into my black converse.

I decide to leave my hair down and apply only minimal makeup. I line my eyes with mascara and put some chapstick on my lips. Hopefully, we're not going anywhere super fancy or I'm going to be severely underdressed.

I make my way back into the bedroom and see Lincoln coming out of the closet. He's got on a pair of dark jeans with a white button-up shirt. He looks so handsome and I'm glad to see that he's not wearing a suit or something dressier.

"You look beautiful, my love." He says as he walks across the room to me.

"You look nice yourself."

"Are you all ready to go?"

"Yeah, I just wanted to grab my purse."

He follows me down the stairs and I grab my purse off of the counter. He takes my hand and leads me to the door. He opens the door for me and I step outside. The view that is in front of me is so unexpected that I freeze.

Parked in front of the house is a carriage, pulled by the most beautiful horse that I have ever seen. My mouth gapes as I stare at them sitting there.

"Is this for us?" I ask.

"Yes."

Lincoln takes my hand and leads me down the stairs where the carriage driver hops down and opens the door for us. Lincoln helps me up and inside before he follows after me. I hop down on the plush seat and look around. The inside of the carriage is covered in purple velvet and I can't stop looking around, trying to take it all in.

We start to move down the street and I smile as I listen to the clip-clop of the horse's hooves. I look over to Lincoln and see that he's just staring at me. He smiles when my eyes meet his and leans over, wrapping his arms me.

"This is awesome." I say as I look up at him.

"I'm glad you like it, love. You know that all I want is to make you happy."

"You do."

"I love you, Adeline. So much."

I want to say it back to him but suddenly the carriage stops and I look outside to see that we're in front of some tall building. Lincoln holds his hand out to me and I take it as he helps me down.

"Where are we going?" I ask.

"Up." He says as he leads me into the building and up the stairs.

We climb up the stairs until we get to a door. Lincoln opens it and leads me out onto a rooftop. The building has been redone with a modern edge to it all. There's cooper pipes and wood everywhere and in the center of it all is a table set up for two. Two waiters stand off to one side, ready to take our orders.

Lincoln leads me over to the table and pulls out one chair for me. He kisses my head before he rounds the table and drops down into his own chair. The waiters step forward and place a chocolate milkshake on the table between us. I laugh as I lean forward and wrap my lips around a straw. Lincoln's pupils dilate as he watches me suck up some milk-shake.

The waiter come over and place two plates in front of us.

"Pizza?" I ask.

"It's your favorite, right?"

"Yes."

"Did you want something else? I can have them make something else if you want."

"No, this is perfect."

I smile at him as I pick up my slice of pizza and bite in. The warm cheese and sauce melts in my mouth. I moan as I take another bite. We talk and admire the view as we finish our food. Lincoln leads me back downstairs once we're done and we climb back into the carriage and head home.

"So?"

"So, what?" I ask.

"How was our first date? How did I do?"

"Best date that I've ever been on. Well, the only date I've ever been on but still, it was perfect."

I lean across the seat and kiss him. What starts as a simple kiss, soon turns into a heated make-out session. I don't see any of the return trip since our lips remain connected the entire time. The carriage stops abruptly and we're jostled back to reality. We pant as we both look at each other, grinning like lunatics.

"I love you, Adeline." He says, cupping my face.

"I love you too."

## LINCOLN

"I love you too."

My mind can't seem to comprehend anything else. Adeline loves me. My entire world is complete. I help her out of the carriage and tip the driver before we head inside. I open the door for us and as soon as I close and lock it behind us, I'm on her.

I press her against the wall, next to the door as I ravish her mouth. I waste no time, slipping my hands under her shirt and my tongue in her mouth. She moans into my mouth and I feel her tiny fingers trying to undo the buttons on my shirt. I let out an impatient growl as I let go of her and my hands come to my shirt. I grip each side and rip, buttons go flying, pinging into corners of the room.

She moans as her hands come back to my chest. She runs her hands up and down my chest and it feels like heaven. She drags her short nails down my arms as she pushes my shirt all of the way off.

I grip her hips and lift her. Her hands wrap around my neck as her legs encircle my waist. I turn and carry her up the stairs. Her lips trail down from my lips to my neck and I feel her bite my collarbone.

I groan as she licks the spot with her tongue.

We stumble into the bedroom and I walk over to our bed, laying her out on it. Her hair fans out around her head and she looks up at me with hooded eyes. Her purple eyes look like they're glowing in the moonlight.

I tilt my head down to hers and brush a kiss across one cheek. I kiss over to her ear as I work her shirt up. She sits up and lets me tug it off over her head before she lays back down. She slides her bra off next and then we're both topless.

I look over her as she lays spread out before me. Her tits are round and topped with rosy pink nipples. As I stare, they harden into tight peaks and I lick my lips, picturing having them in my mouth.

As I watch, she slides her hand up her stomach and cups her breasts for me. I can't wait any longer and my head dips as I lick one tight bud before I take it in my mouth. I suck on it hard before biting it lightly. She moans and arches under me as I continue my ministrations and move to the other one.

She writhes under me and I switch between them until I feel her fingers tugging on my jeans.

"I want to feel you, Lincoln. All of you." She pants.

I stand up and quickly shed my jeans and boxers. She leans up on her elbows to take me in. Her eyes widen as she sees my red cock pointing angrily at her. I'm bigger than most but I already know that my girl is a virgin.

I reach one hand down and wrap it around my length, slowly stroking up and down while she watches. A drop of precum forms on the head and she licks her lips as I continue to touch myself. She sits up and slowly brings her hand to mine, wrapping it around my own and stroking my cock with me.

I let my hand go and she continues to slowly slide her hand up and down my length. I look down at her as she sits up further and leans over me. Then, I feel her warm, wet mouth as it wraps around my tip. I tense as I try not to come immediately. Her tongue licks up and down my pulsing shaft before she wraps her lips around me once again.

She takes me in deep, over and over, swallowing around me each time and I can feel the familiar tingle in the base of my spine. I dig my hands into her hair, gently pulling her off of me.

"Your turn." I say as I lay her down in the center of the bed.

I help her untangle her jeans from her legs and tug her panties down before she settles back. I grip her ankle and spread her legs wide before I crawl up the bed between them. My face is eye level with her center and I know that she wants to cover herself.

"You're so beautiful." I say as I lean forward and use two fingers to spread her lips. Her pretty pink center is wet and inviting and I can't wait another second. I lean forward and lick. Her back arches and I lay my forearm over her hips to keep her steady while my other hand holds her pussy open for me. I lick up her center over and over again and her cries get louder and louder and her orgasm climbs to new heights. My hips hump the bed but my cock knows what it really wants. I just need her to come once before I let him get in her.

I focus my tongue on her hard-little pearl and I circle it, pressing harder and harder on her button until she shatters under me. She cries out and I slide up her body and push inside her as she's at the peak of her pleasure. I'm hoping that she won't notice the pinch of pain this way.

I thrust in to the hilt and hold my hips against hers as she rides out her orgasm and any pain that she might be feeling. She finally opens her eyes and looks up at me. I search her face for any pain but all I see is pleasure. Pleasure and love.

"I love you, Adeline."

"I love you, too."

I lean down and mold my lips to hers as I start to rock in and out of her. I start with shallow thrusts but soon she's gripping my ass and urging me to go harder, faster. I'm a slave to her wishes and my pace picks up. Soon, I'm slamming into her as her hips rise to meet my punishing rhythm.

"Linc, oh Linc. I'm so close." She pants.

"Me too, love. Come for me. We'll come together."

Her back arches and I thrust deep, rubbing the base of my cock against her. I feel her cream gush between us as she comes and I find my own release inside of her. I catch myself on my elbows so I don't crush her and we lay together in a sweaty, sticky mess, trying to catch our breath.

"Wow." She whispers. "Let's do that again."

I laugh as I roll her on top of me and she starts to move.

# CHAPTER TWELVE

## Adeline

It's the night after Lincoln and my date and Aspen and I are out for a girl's night. We decided that we hadn't seen each other enough since she got back from her honeymoon and so we planned a night out.

We started the night with dinner and a movie and now we're at some club. We've been dancing for about half an hour and I'm starting to get thirsty. I motion to the bar at Aspen and she nods as we make our way over to it. We push through the crowd and then wait for our turn to order some drinks. We've had a couple of drinks already and I'm starting to feel a little loose. I can tell that Aspen is feeling a little inebriated too.

"Just one more, right?" I ask.

Aspen seems to think that this is hilarious and I realize that I've asked her that before we ordered the last three drinks. I start to laugh too and soon we're both leaning on the counter cracking up.

"Ok, I think you two have had enough."

I look up as two arms wrap around me. Lincoln is standing there, holding me up and I look over to Aspen to see that Roman and Flynn have her wrapped up in their arms too.

"Come on, love. Let's get you home."

Roman and Flynn are in front of us and I watch as they practically carry her out of the club and into the back of their town car. Lincoln helps me outside and into the passenger side of his car. We follow them back home and I see Aspen and her men head towards their house.

"Night Addy!" Aspen yells drunkenly.

"Night Aspen!" I slur back.

I laugh as Lincoln carries me into our house and up the stairs. He starts to take off my shoes and pants.

"Oh, round two? Well, technically, round three." I trail off as Lincoln starts to laugh silently. He helps me sir up before dragging my shirt and bra off. He slides one of his shirts on over my head and helps me get my arms through.

I drop back down onto the bed and watch as he picks up my dirty clothes and shoes and puts them in the hamper.

"Are you coming to bed?" I ask, trying to be seductive.

"I think I'll let you sleep this off before we make love again." He says drily.

He walks into the bathroom and comes out with a clean washcloth. He lays it on my forehead and I smile sleepily up at him.

"I love you, Lincoln." I say as I drift off to sleep.

## LINCOLN

I never get tired of hearing her say that. I cover her with our comforter and kiss her forehead as I watch her chest rise and fall. I go into the bathroom and get some water and Tylenol for her. With how much she drank tonight, she's going to need it tomorrow.

I'm just about to leave the room when her phone rings. I had plugged it into the charger for her and I look at the screen to see it's Bianca calling her. Bianca worked at the coffee shop with Aspen and the three girls are still close. It's late for her to be calling and before I can second guess myself, I pick it up and answer the call.

"Bianca? It's Lincoln, Adeline is asleep. Are you ok?"

"No." She cries and instantly I'm in protective mode. I may not know this girl, but she's important to Adeline and I would do anything to make sure that she is happy.

"What's wrong?"

"There's this guy. He asked me out and I said yes but then when we did get out, he was just so boring. Just kept talking about his family money and bragging about dumb stuff. He asked me out again but I said no and he hasn't been taking it well. I think he's stalking me. I've seen him following me and he comes into the coffee shop every day still. I don't know what to do."

"Where are you now?" I can hear street noise in the background.

"I ran down to the store to get some cold medicine and I think I just saw him. I'm scared to leave and walk home. Is there any way that you could come and walk me home? Adeline told me you run a security company and I just, I didn't know who else to call."

"My partner is close to where you live. His name is Bryson. I'm going to send him to make sure you get home safe. He's 6'2", blond hair, blue eyes, probably wearing a black t-shirt. I'm texting him now so he should be there in a couple of minutes but I'm going to stay on the line with you until he gets there."

"Ok. Thank you." She sniffs.

I'm not sure how much is from the cold and how much is because she's upset. I send Bryson a quick text, letting him know what's going on and he says he's on his way. I stay on the line with Bianca until I hear Bryson in the background, introducing himself to her.

"Ok, Bianca, Bryson will make sure you're safe. You're in good hands."

"Thank you."

I hang up the phone and go back to my girl. She's still asleep and I smile down at her as I watch her sleep. I go downstairs to take the puppies out one more time before slipping into bed beside my love.

I wake the next morning to Adeline's groans. I sit up and hand her the Tylenol and water and she smiles gratefully at me as she swallows both.

"How are you feeling, love?"

"Like death."

"The medicine will kick in soon. I can take care of the puppies. Why don't you lay down and get some more sleep? I can bring you something to eat in a little bit?"

"That sounds amazing." She says as she finishes the glass of water.

I rub her back as she sits up in bed and that's when I see her phone.

"Bianca called last night. Seems she's got a not so welcome admirer. I was going to head into the office today and try to dig into him a little bit. Are you going to be ok?"

"Is she ok?" She asks, panicked.

"Yeah, I had Bryson walk her home and make sure she was safe."

"Ok, yeah, I think I'll just be sleeping today so go make sure she's ok. I love you." She says as she lays back down.

"I love you too."

I tuck her in before tugging on some clothes and backing out of the room. My girl is already back asleep and I smile as I close the door behind me.

I pull my phone out of my pocket as I walk

down the stairs. I shoot a text to Bryson to see how last night went and to let him know that I'm going to dig into Bianca's stalker today. I hook the dogs up and take them outside to go to the bathroom. They're on real puppy food now and not having to feed them bottles has been amazing. They're almost all the way potty trained now too. We just need to decide what we're doing with all of them. I love Adeline and if she wants to keep them all then I'm on board. It's just not very practical.

My phone buzzes as I'm putting their food down. I pull it out to see that Bryson has responded.

**Bryson:** I've got it covered. Enjoy the day with your girl.

I smile at the phone, sending back a quick thanks before I shove the phone away and head back upstairs to check on Adeline.

# CHAPTER THIRTEEN

## Lincoln

I help Adeline bring the puppies in. I know that this is hard for her but we both agreed that having eight dogs is too much. She decided to keep Quiche, like I knew she would, and Aspen and the boys adopted Mowgli and Bianca is going to take Naia. I think it's easier knowing that they'll have good homes and she'll be here to check out anyone else who wants to adopt the others.

We've been together, officially, for one week and I told her I wanted to take her out to celebrate. She laughed at me and said she thinks that usually, you celebrate when you're dating for longer than a week. I told her I didn't care and she finally gave in.

I kiss Adeline goodbye and head for my next stop. A jewelry store a couple of blocks away. I've been designing something that would be perfect for Adeline since the day I saw her picture and it's finally ready.

I picked out a heart-shaped diamond in a silver band with tiny stones in the band. The stones are different gemstones and look like a rainbow. When I flip the box open and look at it, it reminds me so much of Adeline.

She's been through so much, survived so much, and she's still so full of life and light. She is my heart, my entire world, and she deserves a ring that will show that. I close the box and head home to make sure that everything else is set.

I head back to the shelter to pick Adeline up and she smiles as she climbs into the car. She leans across the console and kisses me before I can get any words out.

"Hey, how was work?"

"Good. All of the puppies got adopted today. I got to meet the new owners and they all seemed so sweet. Mac got picked by this family who had the cutest little girl. And Neal,"

She chatters on about each of the puppy's new owners and I'm so glad that she's happy about them finding their forever homes. I know she was a little sad that they couldn't all stay with us.

We pull up in front of our house and I help her out of the car and up the stairs. I open the door and she steps in, stopping instantly as she sees what I set up for us.

There are flowers everywhere. On the floor, tables, stair, and everywhere that doesn't have flowers is covered in candles and rose petals. In the center of the room, is a blanket with a picnic basket set up next to it.

She turns to me with unshed tears in her eyes.

"Happy one-week anniversary?" She asks.

"Yeah. Happy anniversary, love."

I take her hand and lead her over to the blanket. She settles down on one side and I sit closer to her, opening the basket and taking out some fruit and cheese. We eat one course at a time as she tells me more about the puppy's new owners and some changes that are going to happen at the shelter. She looks so happy and I didn't know that it was possible, but I fall even more in love with her at that moment.

"Where's Quiche?" She asks as we finish dessert.

"In his crate. I didn't want him knocking over one of the candles. Let me grab him."

I rise from the blanket and head into the other room to let the puppy out. I scoop him up in my arms and carry him over to her. She takes him from me and cuddles him against her for a minute, stroking his soft fur as he wiggles all over her. I can tell the moment that her fingers touch it. She looks confused as she pulls him away from her to look at what's on his collar.

"Lincoln?" She gasps.

I smile down at her as I unhook the ring from Quiche's collar and hold it out.

"Adeline, I've loved you since the moment I saw you. You make my life better, just by being in it.

I would do anything for you. Move across the street from your best friend, adopt eight dogs, anything. I love you. I'm yours, now and forever, and I would be honored if you would be mine. Will you marry me, my love?"

My breath catches in my lungs as I wait anxiously for her answer. I'm worried that she'll say no, that she'll think that it's too soon, or that we're moving too fast. I know in my heart that she is my one and only and I'm just hoping that she'll see that too.

"Oh, Lincoln. Yes." She says softly and my heart feels so full that I think it might burst.

"Adeline." I say as I tackle her and Quiche to the blanket.

She laughs as tears slide down her cheeks. I would be worried about the tears but she has the biggest smile on her face and I know that she's happy. There's so much love shining from her eyes and it's directed all at me. I don't know how I got so lucky but I will spend every day for the rest of my life, making sure that she is always this happy.

"I love you Adeline."

"I love you too, Lincoln."

I slide the ring on her finger and we kiss. My lips have barely touched hers when she's yelling and slipping out from under me. I watch as she scoops up Quiche before he can knock over a candle and burn the house down.

"Maybe we should blow the candles out now?"

"Yep." I say, as I stand up to do just that.

I blow out all of the candles while she holds onto Quiche. When the last one is out, she places him back down and he goes after some of the flowers. I sigh as I watch him make a mess before I turn back to Adeline to see her running at me. She launches her tiny body at me and I catch her just in time.

I laugh as her lips meet mine. God, I love this girl.

# CHAPTER FOURTEEN

## Adeline

Aspen comes up to me as I look around the party. All of my friends and family came to celebrate our engagement and we're currently spread out over the kitchen and living room in our house.

"Congratulations!"

"Thanks." I say as she wraps me up in a hug.

"I'm so happy for you."

I hug her tighter as I hear the emotion in her voice. I'm happy for both of us. We finally got our happily ever after's. We have great men who love us and would do anything for us and we still get to live close to each other.

We break apart as I feel someone wrap their hand around my waist and pull me backward. I don't even need to look to know who it is. Lincoln has been glued to my side as we've gone around and talked to everyone.

His mom and dad are here and I finally got to meet them. I was nervous that they would think we were rushing things but they assured me that they had known about me for a while. Apparently, Lincoln couldn't stop talking about me and how he was going to marry me one day. We spent about half an hour talking with them and I promised that we would get together for dinner soon. They only live about an hour outside of the city and I can already picture spending holidays at their home in the country.

Lincoln invited some of the people that work for him at his security company but I've already forgotten their names. They all looked similar with military and dark-colored button-up shirts.

The only one I remember is Bryson Thatcher and that's only because Lincoln has mentioned him a couple times before. Oh, and because he's been glued to Bianca's side.

Even know, I look over and see him trailing around the party after her. He glares at Flynn's brother, Ryan, and I want to laugh. He's treating her the exact way that Lincoln was with me.

"Looks like Bianca might be the next one getting married." I say to Aspen and Lincoln.

"To who?" Aspen asks.

I point over to where Bianca is with her shadow and we watch them for a minute. Bianca is talking with Ryan and Bryson just keeps getting closer and closer to her. I can see Bianca fighting a smile so I know she's aware of how he's crowding her. She doesn't seem to mind though.

"Maybe he's just keeping an eye on her? He is supposed to be keeping her safe until we can get a handle on her stalker situation." Lincoln says.

Aspen and I both snort at that.

"Look at him, babe. He's hooked. That's way more than just doing his job. She's surrounded by family and friends. Her stalker isn't going to get in here, so there's no reason for him to be on top of her like that. Unless he wants to be. "

Lincoln looks back to his friend who now has his hand at the small of Bianca's back as she continues to ignore him and talk to Ryan.

"Maybe you're right." He mumbles. "I wonder if I should take him off her case."

"Why?"

"He's there for her safety and he might get distracted if he's chasing after her."

"Would you ever let anything hurt me?"

"Absolutely not."

"I think he feels the same way. Leave them alone. Nothing is going to touch her. Not with Bryson standing next to her."

"Alright, Mrs. Hook. Have it your way."

I laugh, tuning in his arms as Aspen walks off to find her men.

"I'm not Mrs. Hook yet, you know?"

"Soon, my love."

"I love you, Lincoln."

"I love you more, Adeline."

"I never thought I'd get this."

"Get what?"

"A happily ever after. When my parents died it felt like my future did too. Then, the brain tumor and not being able to afford the surgery, well, I thought I was going to die, but here I am. It feels like a miracle."

"Maybe it was. I know one thing. You're my miracle."

He leans down and kisses me and I know that no matter what comes at me, that Lincoln will be right by my side, ready to love and protect me through everything.

# THE END.

**Look for Bianca and Bryson's story!**

**Pretty Girl is coming soon!**

# ALSO BY SHAW HART

Making Her His
Trouble
Her Obsession
His Obsession
Baby Mama
Bought and Paid For
His Miracle
Pretty Girl
Stopping at Nothing
The Billionaire's Bet
Mine to Love
Mine to Protect
Mine to Cherish
Mine to Keep
Her Guardian Angel
His Firework
My Girl
Every Tuesday Night
His Wish

# CONNECT WITH ME!

If you enjoyed this story, please consider leaving a review on Amazon or any other reader site or blog that you like. Don't forget to recommend it to your other reader friends.

If you want to chat with me, please consider joining my VIP list or connecting with me on one of my Social Media platforms. I love talking with each of my readers. Links below!

- Follow me on Facebook
- Follow Shaw Hart on Bookbub
- Join my private reader group, Shaw Hart Bookies
- Join my VIP list
- Follow me on Instagram

Made in the USA
Lexington, KY
26 November 2019

57730208R00063